Annette Cairnie is an author born in the heart of Europe, in a small country called Slovakia. She developed her passion for writing very early in her life and began to actively write poetry when she was in her teenage years. Annette decided to share her first work with the world when she was only eighteen years old. She's previously written many stories and poems but *Apricity* is the first collection to be published. Cairnie also produces poetry in Slovak and Czech languages.

Dedicated to the little boy who has grown to become the muse for this book.

Annette Cairnie

APRICITY

Austin Macauley Publishers

LONDON · CAMBRIDGE · NEW YORK · SHARJAH

Copyright © Annette Cairnie 2024

The right of Annette Cairnie to be identified as author of this work has been asserted by the author in accordance with sections 77 and 78 of the Copyright, Designs and Patents Act 1988.

All rights reserved. No part of this publication may be reproduced, stored in a retrieval system, or transmitted in any form or by any means, electronic, mechanical, photocopying, recording, or otherwise, without the prior permission of the publishers.

Any person who commits any unauthorised act in relation to this publication may be liable to criminal prosecution and civil claims for damages.

A CIP catalogue record for this title is available from the British Library.

ISBN 9781035835232 (Paperback)
ISBN 9781035835249 (ePub e-book)

www.austinmacauley.com

First Published 2024
Austin Macauley Publishers Ltd®
1 Canada Square
Canary Wharf
London
E14 5AA

Table of Contents

Prologue	11
Part One: Of Holiday and Honeymoon	13
No Air	15
Red Highlights	16
Frameless Glasses	17
Mug	19
Bonfire (An Ode)	20
Skeleton	22
The Seed	23
Veins for Routes	24
That's How I Knew	25
Scotsman	26
Bouncy Castle	27
Bedroom Talks (Confessions)	28
Sweetheart	29
Oh, Sweetheart	30
God Jesus Christ	31
Sweetheart	32

Part Two: The Irreversible Fall — 33

Reading William (Gloomy Friday) — 35
McDonald — 37
Explorer — 38
Visitor — 39
Yellow and Blue — 40
Knowing You (Enlightenment) — 41
Robe Without Chains — 42
Anatomist — 43
Trapped — 44
Morning Breath — 45
Doe Eyes — 46
Lovers' Visit to America (A Story) — 47
The Beginning — 49
Eleven — 50
My Boy — 51

Part Three: Grasping at Straws — 53

Gazelle's Lullaby — 55
Worlds — 56
Learning to Walk (Wanting to Run) — 57
Actor — 58
Nevertheless Mortal — 59
Role-Play — 60
Penetration — 61
Typeface (About Wives) — 62

Part Four: Homecoming	**65**
Ballad of the Pole Dancer	*67*
Politics of Glasgow	*69*
Aunts and Demons	*70*
Over Grave	*71*
But love	*72*
Man on the Bus (First Part of the Story)	*73*
Waiter (Second Part of the Story)	*74*
Cameleer (Third Part of the Story)	*75*
Brown Glass Bottles	*76*
Stupid Word Game	*77*
Part Five: April Child (Second Breathing)	**79**
April Starts Well	*81*
Sunshine Boy	*82*
Mould Me	*83*
Bed of Dandelions	*85*
Seashore	*86*
Her	*87*
Outside of Me	*88*
The Tube	*89*
Messages	*90*
Red Nights and Yellow Days	*91*
Ocean Alley	*92*
Homesick	*93*
Splinter (By the Campfire)	*95*

On My Own	96
Everything (Ineffable)	97
Spider Webs	98
Crook of My Neck	99
No Air (Part Two)	100
Part Six: The Rest of My Life	**103**
Cavemen	105
Soulmate (Not a Self-Poem)	107
Age of Love	108
Under Ground	109
Sundays and TV	111
Laws of Time and Space	112
Imprint	113
Epilogue	**114**

Prologue

There most certainly is a desire within me which requires for my poetry to be great. Appreciated and applauded! No matter how often I said I don't care for it. It is a lot more important to me that I am satisfied with the final writings *myself* rather than seeking admiration in other people, that is true. But deep within I know I need to receive some sort of positive notice from the public as well.

What leaves you wanting others to understand and adore your words is the fact you write about *certain someone* that you deeply care about therefore you can't afford to misinterpret them. To me – I am convinced in my passion and drive when it comes to writing and feel very committed towards my work. That is mainly because I write about a person I love and value and when you find yourself entirely dipped into a feeling like that, you begin to think there is no more you can possibly feel. No better structure of a poem you can come up with. I felt everything, when I wrote, with every atom of my body. So, who could ever write better than those who feel so profoundly so much? Every author wants to get the very best out of their work because if they wrote badly, it would simply mean they do not know nor feel enough. They want everyone to see how much love and devotion they put into the combination of words they choose.

So yes, I ache for my poetry to be interpreted as well-written. I need *them* – those I write about – to be no other but well-written.

Part One
Of Holiday and Honeymoon

No Air

You kiss me so delicate
Imprisoning the air between your mouth and mine
First you brush me just so lightly
As if but a landing butterfly
Then you start painting holy bruises across my lips
And your eagle nose carves destinies into my cheek
I don't want to let go
Because once you pause my breathing
That's when I begin to feel alive

(February 8th 2023)

Red Highlights

Your gentle hands touch me all over
And they're so divine I can barely feel them
But I see them
They're like a sand dune in slow-motion
They're all the beaches
Warmed by the southern sun
I dive my fingers into the soft matter
The auburn strands growing from your nape
I've run them about a million times
I'd do a million and one more All I know
Is all I am when I'm with you
All I know
Is the sun creating red highlights in your hair?
As we make love
All I know
I found a place for my broken bones to settle
And it's warm
It's beautiful

(February 9th 2023)

Frameless Glasses

Everything was pastel yellow
And the weather was alright for February
You had your frameless glasses on
And, God, I used to hate those
The room was filled with fragments of you Memories I
didn't think I owned so, do I know you?
A minute?
A month?
Or nine hundred and thirty-nine weeks?

I'm beginning to learn your structure
Your habits
Your heart
Don't tell me I'm not where I'm supposed to be
Because my name's already on the post box

I can live inside of you
And you can live inside of me
In a light blue house on a cliff
Big enough to let us breathe
Small enough to keep us close

Knitted pillows on the sofa
And your glasses left at the coffee table

(February 9th 2023)

Mug

You took your mug with you as we went for a walk
Just outside the house and round the cliffs
And I found it strange
How quickly things change their form
I watched you ignore all of reality
Just so you could spend some time with me

My plates have never left my house
And a month ago I'd label you a loony but we walked
And the shore breeze caressed my face
Everything felt peaceful

It will take a while for me to get my mug outside
But until the day comes
I can always have a sip from yours

(February 10th 2023)

Bonfire (An Ode)

I love everything you do to me
Everything you do to my body
Everything you do to my head
My skin's like heated roof under your touch
And I burn
Like a bonfire so wide and free
Love is here with me
It lies between your lips and the inside of my thigh
I'm out of place
I'm out of breath
I shiver head to toes
Like a birch moved by the wind
I love you
So heavily I might believe
I've not loved anyone before

I'm on fire
And the flame in me is you
I love you
Like tomorrow's not to come
All of world is in your eyes

To making love
To being yours
To your breath falling down on me
To your mouth swallowing my fears
My doubts
To feeling you
To feeling myself flicker away

(February 13th 2023)

Skeleton

Your skeleton's as if made of eggshells
Nothing but a pair of paper-thin wings
Your face is just some cheekbones covered in skin
Your jaw a blade
I loved kissing your bones
I loved touching your skull
Diving into your eyes –
Two dark absorbent black holes
Nothing but a universe

(February 15th 2023)

The Seed

Something's planted in me
It blooms
It's beautiful
I decay but it keeps growing
My body vanishes but the heart's being fed you've come at eleventh hour
Soon I will be gone but the garden remains
Soon you'll be the only thing left of me

(February 17th 2023)

Veins for Routes

There are veins on your neck
And they're like a map of a world
I've not known before
I want to travel all the places
I want to go far in this world
Follow your bloodstream
For it's a path I should've taken a long time ago

(February 19th 2023)

That's How I Knew

My eyes glazed
Because, darling, you seemed so happy
That was the first time I cried out of proudness
And I didn't think it would feel so significant
For the first time someone else's smile
Meant more to me
Than anything I could possibly dream into this life
That's how I knew
That's when I realised
I hardly saw you through the blur
But we cried and smiled together
You were happy and that's all that mattered
It'd made me realise
I don't care what happens to me
As long as you don't know harm

(February 19th 2023)

Scotsman

You throw your *r*'s like tiny needles
And they pin onto my spine
I can feel you in my flesh
The vibration of your voice
Sliding down my back
It's like an early morning sex
Like the very last drop of water after showering
I believe you touch me when you speak
Your voice wraps my throat
Like a hand of a murderer
It tightens
Worth dying for
A single word of yours

(February 20th 2023)

Bouncy Castle

The bouncy castle's falling down
It covers us in patches of all colour
Red
Yellow
Blue
Hiding our tender bodies from the sight of this world
Underneath the warmed-up plastic
I press myself into you
And you do as well
When I think of our love
I think of it exactly like that
Like the moment I saw the sunshine cut your eyes like a razor blade Careless
Unpredictable
With a taste of a childlike mind
That hasn't yet been murdered by the mighty hands of reality

(February 21st 2023)

Bedroom Talks (Confessions)

Words mumbled into my forehead
Like a prayer
Tender fingertips circle my shoulder
I fell in love with the sound of your breath
It's bad

I cannot think of a matter more worthy to crawl into
Than the freckled skin you already wear so well

I live for the sound of your laughter when you're tired
The aftertaste of your gentle kisses
And the echoes they leave
I love the golden lightning of our bedroom
That swallows your face

You're falling asleep
But your heart's reading me sonnets like a bedtime story
You're falling asleep
But I will remain awake until the night knocks me out
Admiring your everything won't ever tire me

(February 22nd 2022)

Sweetheart

Careful tiny sighs of pure ecstasy
Reverberate through the room
Whimpers bumping into walls mindlessly
An everlasting theme of delight with a rhythm so steady
As my heart when we're together

Oh, Sweetheart

You're calling me
Adding a special tail in the form of a whine to the last syllable
And I melt into the sound of it
One would bawl

God Jesus Christ

But you chose to call for me
Over any holy man

Sweetheart

I could write hundreds of poems about that howl of yours

(February 23rd 2023)

Part Two
The Irreversible Fall

Reading William (Gloomy Friday)

I am trying to understand Shakespeare
For the man singing silly lullabies to his children
You've grown over great literature
You know more of the world
And I most certainly don't speak Elizabethan
It only gives sense to try for you

I am reading this bloke William
Underlining all sentences in which you hide
And there's truth to his words
As well as there's truth to mine

You may be happy alongside me
But you won't be well
Now go and feed the children some other woman blessed you with
For I am only destined to burn until I'm ashes
I won't be the mother to your issue we won't share a gravestone
But in my mind I'll hold your hand
You'll sing to me

Sometimes it happens to be true
There are loves which are designed to only exist in theory

(February 24th 2023)

McDonald

Let's talk of painkillers
Abandoned Facebook profiles covered in dust
And low-quality photographs
Let's talk of the beauty in privacy
And your maiden name
Buzzing in my teeth like the sweet bitterness of ripe lemon
I'm writing a letter like it didn't rain yesterday
And although you and I are both human
Made of bones and flesh
Flaws and virtues
I orbit you like a moth does a light bulb
And love like I've only just come into this world

(February 26th 2023)

Explorer

Countless grains of sand flow within your complexion
Wisdom of centuries
You could be a newborn or a retiree
Not known of age is your soul
It smiles from your eyes like a schoolboy cheerful and merry
I know exactly what I look for
And what I don't
I will attempt to like anyway
I dug my hands too into the sand I became unaware of the heat
I watched your skin flare
And didn't care if it would burn my eyes

Visitor

What a vision
Full of delight and grace you lay
In your white shirt rip opened
An authentic copy of Thomas Jerome Newton
Bleached locks even whiter under the pale light of the moon
The structure of your physiognomy as sharp and as striking
as ever
An anthemic way about you
Uplifts my distress
Excites me utterly
A moment so hasty a brush wouldn't catch it, what a shame!
Here's a poem revering your dark rainy eyes
You, my only muse

(February 27th and 28th 2023)

Yellow and Blue

The moon was like a smudge
A stain of spilled yellow spreading across the midnight sky
And I thought of you as the hundreds of city lights lightened
up
As the thousands of heads went to bed
I swear I felt your arms wrap around me
Whispering lustful things into my ear
which under the blanket of the night didn't seem as filthy
I tasted Marlboro
And your clean mouth
As I stepped closer to the window
The clouds parted swiftly
There was the moon
Sharp
Rich
No longer vague

(February 27th 2023)

Knowing You (Enlightenment)

Let me kiss you across your appendicitis scar
Let me notice your heavy eyelid as if for the first time
It's been two fortnights yet they felt like years
No one could identify you as promptly
Yet you're still but a restless dream
I cannot take for granted
Let you teach me how to read
I only read fuming bitter lips all this while
I shall decorate the nitrogen in my air with everything you taught me
And what I once feared would bring such pain
Has cleaned my lungs eventually, the life is changed
Let me know you for the rest of it

(March 2nd 2023)

Robe Without Chains

As an atheist
Can I learn the names of saints in less than a night?
For I am eager to find yours upon that list
Starry eyes and steady hands
Majestic creature
You're the angel inviting me to dream
You stole the stillness of the day
Pronounced it your own
How do you know so much?
While I don't even know a way to call you?
Seductive yet innocent and virginal, what is it now that I believe?
The gold's glory and bliss or the purity of sin?
I know so little of the celestial world
Only you

(March 3rd 2023)

Anatomist

Tell me in your language
Fluent in structure of living things
How many books have you slept with before you stumbled across me?
Lesson me on my muscles and my nerves
Instruct me through this terrible age of life
When everyone seems to open locks but leave the gate closed
I want someone to know me better than I know myself
Now I know it's possible

(March 3rd 2023)

Trapped

As Orlando did for Rosalind
I too carved your name and my poems
Into bark of every tree
I did
I did it but in an infinite forest
And you're not a bird or a wolf
You've never seen it here

So, I surround myself with rather sorrowful hymns unseen
Questioning
How can something infinite make me feel so trapped?

(March 6th 2023)

Morning Breath

Tired eyes not yet clothed in contacts
Looked at me soaked into the dry purple skin
Lips parted and the breath nowhere near fresh

What dreams have put sweat upon your forehead?
How long until you recognise me and smile?

I felt the weight of your lashes
And it made me want to dive into the sheets
I know I can rest here
And be a corpse yet living with you
So does it make me a loon?
If I counted freckles on your arm while you were sleeping?
If I measured out your hair?

I was always meant to get this far in being
To witness the slice of daylight tracing your grey shirt
I live because life is hidden in its simplest whiles

(March 6th 2023)

Doe Eyes

I promised myself one day I was going to write about your
doe eyes
And how your cheekbones carry them like a sled
There was the poem today
Written right within the iris as I looked into them

With a body made of puzzled tiles
And a voice escaping it
As if knocking of a glass marble
The does ran down the forest
As millions of marbles traced their shy serene footsteps
The nature smelled of you
The river streams formed a template of your bod
Spring has left its babes at the door
Little sparks of rebirth

And a very fawn of our own
My deer Doe-Eye
I think the leaves have grown back specifically for us

(March 7th 2023)

Lovers' Visit to America (A Story)

There they go
Two lovebirds on a bike in pouring rain
One dressed in a suit and a tie
Too much black for a fair pale Northerner
And she – like a peony in bloom
Was old enough to see the film they played in cinema
But too juvenile to look her fellow traveller in the eye
And so, they stared forward
Desperate to find each other's fingers in the darkness of their blindfolds
Even a simple breath would break the tension
But they were holding it so still

Lovers in the sunset
Chasing seagulls like they're a promising tomorrow
And when the setting's done
The small-town boy who vowed to go to the North Pole for her
Is dancing off his heart in his Presley collar
And a ducktail
To the tune of his peony's footsteps
As she's leaving with the sun

He rescued the dress she was wearing the day they met
And clothed himself in the fabric remembering her perfume
Remembering
That evening in the cinema –
And now the memory's vividly recovered – He couldn't take his eyes off of her
She was the one fearful to look

The Beginning

We held hands through the veil
Walked on the opposite sides of the road
You were in the room exactly thirty-eight seconds before me
I could still feel you there
I just didn't know it was you
You're the person sitting in the fourth row
Watching my labour
You were always here

(March 7th 2023)

Eleven

Fairest of creatures
Yet with her feet tied to the ground
They have walked twice the distance mine have
She's only been around a decade but still I stared
Longer than I should
At things I shouldn't be staring at
These late-night hours do this to me

I found your lips upon her face
Your nose growing from its centre
I see you
Twenty-three
Equal to eleven
Oh, but her eyes uncover a different story
I cannot wait to hear it in your narration
I will watch you grow all over again once more before I'm
set to go
Won't miss a year now I've got to pay attention
I will witness every wrinkle added to her face

(March 11th 2023)

My Boy

My boy can jump really high
And with every landing he makes the ground quiver
Underneath my feet
He moves like a shadow
In spaces lacking light
As weightless as the flight of a feather he's the breath laid
upon the back of my neck

My boy has the sweetest sense of excitement
He's as constant as a transient
A poem memorised from years ago
A formula learnt by heart
Commanded by heart to learn

My boy has the ability to leave me speechless for days
No words conquer him
And so empty my mind feels when I look at him
Heart tremendously full
My boy needs to be written with patience and slowly

To touch a silky stream of air
Be a ghost or be a myth
I will feel the Earth move in your rhythm anyway
And dance to it as if it's my duty

(March 11th 2023)

Part Three
Grasping at Straws

Gazelle's Lullaby

When your eyes were the size of the moon
Too wide too dreamy for a face to disguise
Like a gazelle shot but not wounded
You were never the prey

Good hunter laid his palm on my bleeding lesion
Knew one look into the angelic face would cure every bruise
not yet made Every time you leave a wound you come
kissing it for me within seconds

How long has the sweet pain of your arrows been putting me
to sleep?
There was a stare of a victim peeking through the thin air
Fond but sharp
Razor-like yet affectionate all at once
I let it be my lullaby
And now I suck on my own blood before I sleep
Hunter in my dreams
Gazelle to my eyes
And all through and through
Flawless
(March 13th 2023)

Worlds

I'd like to see the world end
The ending of the life I lived in your touch
Knowing I'll be closing my eyes for the final time
And you shall be the last of things I ever see
Stars crashing our skin like a downpour of dusty teardrops
until it melts our consciousness away, will we remember?
A moment like this
Everything we felt on our life's pilgrimage
I want to retain the warmth you've inserted to my flesh
The rousing and rather boiling feeling I can't undo from my blood
Let me take it to every life to come
For I want to find you in each of them
And take care of you through worlds

(March 13th 2023)

Learning to Walk (Wanting to Run)

I'm learning to walk while I've known to run
I'm kissing the lips telling me I'm not a good kisser
Yet they used to shiver of pleasure under mine
Subtle love has set my feet on fire
Interrupting me

Now I'm recovering from severe burns
But I swear I have all the patience in the world
And leisurely
If that's what it takes
Step after step relearnt
I shall experience the wind striking my face from both sides
I put no speed limit to my desire to run

And I'll never stop running
Once I'm back on my feet
I want to feel everything again
To the point it would no longer seem there's anything left to feel

(March 14th 2023)

Actor

You spoke to me in Romeo and I fancied you
You spoke to me in death and I felt the grief
You spoke to me in anger and I feared you
Then you spoke to me in you
And that's my favourite
Because you're all of it
You're the eyes of the sky and the lungs of the soil
I will probably spend the rest of my days trying to figure you out
Understand why that is you amaze me so
To you my life is nothing but a stage
And you're the greatest play of all time

(March 14th 2023)

Nevertheless Mortal

To kiss the blood painted eyelids of the dying
Keep trying to breathe in the very last breath of life
Knowing you won't succeed
Stare at the see-through skin as if it's the finest piece of art
And hold the hand that's soon to be dust
Tight from the moment you first joined in touch

You'd still see the skin as red as a rose late to May
The darkening eyes as full of youth as if they just discovered life
And as the face would dim in turquoise eclipse
You'd see it unchanged
If you ever loved the mind within

(March 14th 2023)

Role-Play

You wrapped your mouth around the word weather
And the tenderness of your scratchy voice set my pulse in motion
I felt once more
The echoing past has never approached me this kindly before
We met for the first time again
And for a minute I pretended not to know the words to your song
You reached out your hand
And like forbidden lovers we introduced ourselves with made up names
So called for the counterfeit appeared to me
But darling
Next time I ask for your name
Tell me the real one

(March 15th 2023)

Penetration

Ask me if I want to slow down
I'd say I wouldn't mind hitting my head on the ceiling of my devotion
Tangle into sheets of eternal togetherness

Ask me if I want to tone down my scratches
I'd say I haven't yet dug my nails deep enough
Because I haven't
Haven't yet started resisting the end

I'd pull your hair even tighter
Hide within you until they'd stop searching
I refuse to let my fingers appear slippery
If the subject matter, is you

Where I should be writing out of love
I write of ire and uneasiness
We deserve better
Than to sit on the outside of each other

(March 15th 2023)

Typeface (About Wives)

This is how I imagine
Peace on Earth and breeze on the beach
Where the clear waves crash the cliffs gently
Nature's love making – secluded and deeply personal

With the way he looked at her
I never wanted him to look at me again
I wrote these verses in her name
So that he could leave his eyes on them instead

Those whose laughs vibrate in sync
Whose features like a puzzle
Form a mosaic
An evergreen
Love her and let her not be loved more by anyone
Treasure him and let me not adore him in greater silence

And in addition
My gratitude
Such sensation

Vastest satisfaction to face a proof of love that's authentic and true
But what's more – powered by laughter

This one is for her
Every of my morning's prayer
Is for you to live up to your desires
Now that mine have been passed onto someone else

(March 15th 2023)

Part Four
Homecoming

Ballad of the Pole Dancer

I see a pole dancer at his peak
With glitter spilled underneath his eyes
Is it glitter?
Or is it tears
Watering his crow's feet?
He's been around a long time now
You can tell by all the colours he reflects
By the number of costumes, he's worn and threw away
Trying to adapt to the ever-changing fashion

The poor face looks up to the sky
Knowing he'd soon have to choose a star to settle in

I'm climbing my way to the top of the planet
So I can hold my pole dancer for one last time
And we hugged
Our chests growing attached
Sweat imprinting glitter on my skin

He's never stripped for simple human minds
And now his naked soul shimmers underneath my touch
You're not a whore

I've never seen a soul this chaste I won't allow you to leave
Feeling like you've lived in shame

(March 16th 2023)

Politics of Glasgow

There you looked like a completely different person
One I knew but never met
With your messy hair and a stubble
Audrey on your T-shirt covered in multiple layers
Smiling and eating and drinking
Doing all the terribly everyday things

Your parents came in through the door with that decorative glass panel
And we talked until the dawn reminded us the night had passed
About your roots
Your teenage years
And the politics of your land which I knew the bare minimum about
I heard the softness in your voice when we mentioned war
I loved seeing you in a light like that
You are home

(March 16th 2023)

Aunts and Demons

The handsome devil blurred the room away
As I invited him with warm laughter of liquor-y tone
An old familiar of mine
Long time no see
She – who was sitting next to me – knew him by name
But what she didn't know
I frequently called it when nights got lonely

What she thought of him
And whether it was good or bad
Remains a mystery
Oh, but it felt so good
Hearing others knew him too
It assured me that he wasn't just a pipe dream of mine

(March 17th 2023)

Over Grave

She died and the love left unused
Sat above her grave Sighing *Will he take us now?*

How could one love a corpse?

The bones shook beneath the ground
Replying

But love

We were a corpse since the moment we realised
We'd never be deserving of his affection

(March 18th 2023)

Man on the Bus
(First Part of the Story)

The man on the bus was wearing his hair half down
While the upper part was wrapped in a thin black rubber tie,
it was carmine – the hair
The only splash of colour to his fully black choice of
dressing
There were no eyes to this man, only stylish sunglasses
Perhaps that was a good thing
Then the buses started flooding the city out of the window
Proper London double decker buses in traditional red
Rushing
Circling our heads as if they were fuelled by lust
The man relaxed himself on the seat
Yellow bus handles framing his face
He was smiling through the whole voyage
Rather mischievous grin upon his face
Sharp teeth and rat-like chops
That my eyes had been resting on for a good minute
And when I decided to break the staring and look around
The bus was empty
Empty all this while

Waiter (Second Part of the Story)

The waiter owning his job for seemingly not too long
Was wearing white for the very first time
Not completely bright
With the usual black smart trousers and a tie
His hair freshly trimmed for the occasion
The occasion being a casual garden party
Family and close friends only
And then waiter

Now he was no longer of elated face
But quite worried, we could say
I tried to get his attention by desperately tracking his paths
with my sight
But without success
Like a Fata Morgana
I was no longer sure who the dreamer was!
And what was the dream?

Cameleer (Third Part of the Story)

Surrounded by flames
He didn't turn into dust but simply disappeared
And if I were to believe in reincarnation
I'd say he became the cameleer in afterlife
I saw him waiting in the queue to heavenly gates for one last time
About three or four people separating us
His brick hair falling down to his shoulder blades now
Thick and lustrous
The Sahara of fog and beige celestial sand made him seem rather corporeal
Human
He lifted his head and looked me straight in the eye
Now I know why he'd never done that before

(March 20th 2023)

Brown Glass Bottles

I sank into the drunken eyes
Which reminded me of the bottom of two brown glass bottles
Mouth underneath whispering *Stay*
And even without asking I'd do
This wasn't the violent insobriety that'd often made me flinch
This was a still promise of beer-flavoured kisses
Tipsy storytelling and hangover laughs

(March 20th 2023)

Stupid Word Game

What is it like?
To get a message everyday
Just one, for a start
From a man unknown of the world of digitalness
Until it is so frequent –
The texting –
It becomes a smooth routine of your day?
Quite a long question to be answered briefly
Or to be answered at all

Your messages have punctuation
Correct grammar
Careful choosing of words in order to express an emotion
Sentences cleverly put together
I wish someone would make such effort to seem so smart
with me
In an activity so ordinary
No, wait
Forget it
I wish your name would appear on my screen today

(March 21st 2023)

Part Five
April Child (Second Breathing)

April Starts Well

In April, we went climbing mountains
Shouted down the open space
As our very own voices echoed
And returned as strangers
We exchanged warm smiles with them
A young couple of lunatics
Thirstful for one another
Their unstained
Genuine hearts filled with want and expectations
It lived within us and yet we never noticed
The gene of a Phoenix
I spent today dancing at the highest point of the mountain
With a voice I just met
And the world kept spinning
And it all came back to me

(April 1st 2023)

Sunshine Boy

Knowing a sunshine boy
Is finding out there's a surprisingly small amount of glow
within his flesh
Realising it's rather about the cosy heat of rain-covered
ground after storm
Like during long steamy August days
When you'd least expect a tempest
And yet they're known to come
The sunshine boy has such a maze of shadow-haunted
chambers inside himself
I know now
People who don't perceive the world solely with their eyes
Find out sunshine isn't just a show of light
It's also the warmth

(April 3rd 2023)

Mould Me

Advise me how you yearn to be loved
So that I may know my rock bottom
Ever-evolving
I'll read every book known to man
Start from there
Your existence has awakened yet another unknown room
within my soul

Let me sleep inside your brain
Let me crawl in there
Study every section of it under the sheets
With a tiny light on

Burn me with your flaming passions
And either light up my spark
Or turn me to ashes
I never want to not know you again
Your grace has stained me too badly
To settle for less of beauty
I would cut mountains at their bottom
And bring them over to your feet
How madly is silent heart capable of loving?

Advise me how to mould my mind
Make me the shape you'd ache for

(April 3rd 2023)

Bed of Dandelions

Then suddenly my bed began to be shaped like your arms
The pillow placed its silken lips on the nape of my neck
It was too late by then
To step away and watch the birth from afar
Too late to set alarm
Not even a bed of roses would've hold my bones more tenderly

Where once wars fired their weapons
Forest rain has grown dandelions
And that night they bloomed like ever
Hugged by the darkness' navy limbs
Life breathed yet fourth time in a row
Leaving me breathless

(April 4th 2023)

Seashore

Silky hips like sea waves
Crash my sand-like bones senselessly
One shall fall in love with the feeling of being drowned
After years and years of droughts
I never thought I'd spend my moonlights sailing down the waters of Eden
Until the bosom of the sea carried me to shore like seashells
Left me there to dry in the pale light of the stars
In the warm coolness of the speechless hours
I know it here
I know but a single ocean
And its ripples trace your voice

(April 4th 2023)

Her

I met the crystal eyes and searched for the hand of envy to bring her to see
But the light of the day turned my good old friend to air
There I was naked
But it's the clothing that makes us foul
She began to undo the buttons of her sleeve
And in matter of seconds
We both stood there– unarmed
It grasped my sense of thinking
Put it out on light
And there I saw that her and I are both just some sack of bones
Minds alike it hurt
Then the corners of my mouth lifted up a bit
But not more than what a bit is worth
I understood we're too similar
Yet still not the same
But oh, I swear I've learnt to love her
And shall never forget I have

(April 4th 2023)

Outside of Me

Two mouths pronounced the same name
And two pairs of eyes caressed the drying paint of a masterpiece
Suddenly I didn't feel so alone in my thoughts
Like when the dark sky sets sparks into one's pupils
There certainly were fireflies in ours

I told my long lost friend everything I thought I knew
About all the reasons and all the days we're given
The dim of evening left me space to open up to the world
And even the February cinders from the very bottom of my lungs
Grains of dust from the day we met
Kissed the span of the outer world
Suddenly you existed
Outside of me

(April 5th 2023)

The Tube

There's a boy on the tube
Wearing glasses broken way too many times
Grasping at his nose not to fall
And I sit opposite his very recognizable eyes

Greetings, lovely dream
I suppose you haven't seen the red carpets yet
The stage lanterns lighting your way to the admiration of many
They'll applaud
They'll be cheering your name
I see it as clear – fellow fever dream –
As I noticed the train going in reverse
One day –
And a great day to come –
You will get there to take over the world
And I will watch
I won't wash the selfless boy off my sight

(April 6th 2023)

Messages

You went for messages
I noticed you at the shops but remained furtive
For your own good
When did it all get this sad?
You – *plural* – went for the messages earlier this evening
So, tell me how could I not be mad?
How am I supposed to not feel every fierce emotion
Entering my wounds like a blade?
And reveal to me how to live my life outside your house
When I've just begun to live because of you

(April 7th 2023)

Red Nights and Yellow Days

Where you wear scars
I place my lips
Where you silence your laughs
I mumble words of a song
I want you to speak at me
I want you to never stop

Do not vanish from my sight
Or my touch
Because there I feel you
Profoundly in my bones
I close my eyes and all's red
You're red nights
And yellow days
I do not know nothing more beautiful

I have you painted on the inside of my eyelids
I have memorised your voice
And there my blood's only you
Let them operate

(April 12th 2023)

Ocean Alley

Remember when I didn't know how to hold you?
Seems surreal
Now I know every vein in your heart
Every book you've ever read
And I recognize you inside myself when I talk to people
Recalling the first ever song I signed your name to
Hearing it today
Sounds nothing like you

(April 13th 2023)

Homesick

To Noel
To Alec
To Gracie
And to all unspoken words
Unshared jokes
Unfelt touches
To times I thought I could've felt more even if I felt it all
Life drives me away from that beach
My toes aren't meant to be dug into that sand
I'm not meant to have the wind hug me from behind
We created a world and we won't leave it shattered
But to leave it abandoned is much more tearful

To your eyes that never looked at me with love
To my mouth never brave enough to call you by name
To every breakfast we've not eaten together
I assume I know what it looks like
The place we tried to build on false hope and aspirations
I knew a beach

And I knew a home
But now I'm leaving it to leave me homesick

(April 13th 2023)

Splinter (By the Campfire)

A little boy ran into my arms
With splinter in his finger
By the campfire they were roasting marshmallows
And as he asked me to blow his pain away
The voice struck me so
It left me feeling faint
I recognized it from years ago
And each of the years lacked two seasons
It must've been spring

I kissed his finger
And he disappeared in a blink of an eye
I wasn't invited to the campfire
I wasn't a part of his life

(April 14th 2023)

On My Own

This love will hold me at gunpoint one day
Threatening
But rather whispering, it'll pull the trigger
Unless I get to live inside of you
As we promised at the beginning
And I get pale
For it's a thing I don't know how to accomplish
I've ran out of ideas how to model the air to be the shape of you
My mind no longer sends the taste of your mouth to my tongue
Very soon this love will divulge my play pretend
It will realize I've been sleeping on my own all this while

(April 15th 2023)

Everything (Ineffable)

Since I've known a breeze softening the rocks
I can no longer bare the scratching wind trying to hold my body down
I've seen brain as if from a surgeon's point of view
Now regular is a grey point of my eye
Nothing but blue skies above my head
It's all so scaringly beautiful
How do you call such thing?
Have they assigned it a name?
Everything
Everything but ugly
But there's still appeal in unappealing
Oh, this must be me
Or it's nearly finished consuming me
It ruined everything for me

(April 15th 2023)

Spider Webs

Maybe you smiled too often the skin around your eyes
decided to keep hugging onto that smile
I'd like to think about it that way
But your neck's getting thinner
It parts in the middle
Your hairline's stepping backwards
Wait
Don't go just yet
Perhaps I'm going to see you in two summers
Would I recognize who you've become?
It's nothing I swear
Aging is not an act of love's
But fear is love's keepsake
And so I fear
I fear arriving home in two years' time
And noticing an announcement across the door
Building soon to be demolished

(April 15th 2023)

Crook of My Neck

Each time your nose makes its way to the crook of my neck
Your mouth lands on my collar bone
Then your eyes flicker through my face as if examining it
I think that's the significant move
I'll remember in connection with you
Won't allow anyone to touch me there the way that you have
And every night I take the shower
Too afraid to wash the spot still wet from your kisses
I want to wear you like a pendant
I want to feel you anyplace I go

(April 15th 2023)

No Air (Part Two)

Oh, first I wrote a poem
But so many things I've left out
I recalled with tonight's moon
The sleek
Nearly silk-like strands sliding down my face
Like a paintbrush layering a wall
As you lowered yourself to my chest

You kiss the way you speak
Passionately
Longingly
Like you've wanted to speak for ages but someone kept
interrupting you
And you rest your head on my shoulder
Because no matter how loudly our eyes are fluent in craving
the other
There's never a rush to whatever that is we have
We've figured that a long time ago
Haven't we?

Today feels like a day I've already known
Today feels like I'm crashing your lips for the first time
I have you
I have you at the tip of my nose
Birds' wings caress my insides
As I let my addiction devour me
The urge to brush my lips against the rose skin of yours is colossal
I don't have to breathe
For as long as my last breath dies inside your mouth

(April 16th 2023)

Part Six
The Rest of My Life

Cavemen

And it's quiet and slow
So soundless you can hear the air fondle the walls of the cave
Inky dark and dim
As deep as the ground reaches
But no loneliness
No solitude
Nor gloom or sorrow
No fear
Rather homely and sheltered
It only allows you to wear the skin of another person on top of your own

Undeniably a mistery
Why we met
Or why it lasts
Why your arms hang around my shoulders
And they're heavy
I let their weight drag me into bed
Where blindly
Uncritically I find your chest

Place my ear on the heated plane
To hear the only sound in my cave

(April 22nd 2023)

Soulmate (Not a Self-Poem)

She'd stay
It's all I demand to know
When the night gets onerous
And the tooth gets broken
Her bosom would become your asylum
And she lacks more hands
For she cannot write
So I do it for her
Her palms too busy wrapping your arm
Numbing your pains
Then how am *I* in use?
Because I want to be
Rather than a cruel echo
Let me be her voice –
That angelic thing
So forbid me to be corporeal
If that permits me to brush your life

(April 22nd 2023)

Age of Love

I think love wore grey zip-up sweatshirt
And walked around the hospital in pyjama pants
Love looked better with beard
But often shaved it clean
Love spoke with food in its mouth
Love had big hands
And frankly skinny legs
And if you'd ever ask me what age love was
Judging by its voice
The enthusiasm in its eyes when that one topic came to words
It couldn't have been older than a decade
And even to assume love is ageless
Would still be better than to know the truth

(April 22nd 2023)

Under Ground

I don't know their voices –
I don't recognize
Disdain the way they talk to me
Or what that is they say
They're but a choir singing in the background

The names I forgot within seconds
The eyes I forgot to pay attention to their colour

One time she mentioned her lovable fiancé and all I thought

–

You
What would you do?
What would you say?
And how'd you say it?
Into every scenario, I draw you precisely without leaving out
a freckle
And it's like a hug from a ghost
I smell of death and repellent people who are not of the same
nature
I rot for you
I rot in waiting

For our bodies to tangle once, they're beneath the soil
I'd crawl my way to you under the ground
I swear to death
As for death is the only certainty

(April 23rd 2023)

Sundays and TV

In a remote town
In one remote living room
Full of remotely desolate people
They were watching a different film than the one projected on my screen
And I can sometimes feel the seclusion nip on my heart
When everything I do doesn't feel like what I should be doing
What I could be
Everything I crave like coffee in the afternoon is remote
And I comprehend
Remote control, in effect, could never control things this remote

(April 23rd 2023)

Laws of Time and Space

I was minus seven when I hugged a boy who claimed he
needed to be hugged
A hint of his cry rang in my yet unborn ear
I hugged him through time and space
Because that's the person I seem to be
While he daydreamed about another arms
I fought my way out of the rip opened womb not yet ripe
Without hesitation
From that moment on I knew I'd just go
Through graves
Through lives
And he liked a girl who as if air walked past his curling guts
While I was gambling with all the laws
For a single sunrise by his side

(April 24th 2023)

Imprint

You couldn't love me so you gave away your fingerprint
Met the tip of my finger
Now people say I've changed
But I love who I've become
When I lay awake, my breathing sounds like yours
The face that catches my attention in the mirror mimics the way you smiled at me for the first time
Imprinted on my tongue –
Every word you said
I won't bother to explain to common people
The glee of assimilating you
You couldn't love me so you just touched me
Proving I am lovable

(April 24th 2023)

Epilogue

Ask me, which is the most painful to write about. Sorrow? Loss? Grief? I've had my answer prepared for some time now; everything, you wanted to feel but didn't.